"And don't let go." — For Cree, always.

Giant Giant

Text and illustration copyright © 2022 by Dylan Hewitt
Copyright © Milky Way Picture Books

All rights reserved.

Book design and typography by Dylan Hewitt
Additional design for this edition by Jolin Masson
Copy editing by Nick Frost

The illustrations in this book were created digitally.
This book was typeset in BorisBlackBloxx.

This edition published in 2022 by Milky Way Picture Books,
an imprint of Comme des géants inc. Varennes, Quebec, Canada.

Library and Archives Canada Cataloguing in Publication

Title: Giant giant / Dylan Hewitt.
Names: Hewitt, Dylan, author. | Hewitt, David (illustrator), illustrator.
Identifiers: Canadiana 20210053801 | ISBN 9781990252082 (hardcover)
Classification: LCC PZ7.1.H49 Gi 2022 | DDC j823/.92—dc23

ISBN 978-1-990252-08-2

Printed and bound in China

Milky Way Picture Books
38 Sainte-Anne Street
Varennes, QC J3X 1R5
Canada

www.milkywaypicturebooks.com

Giant
Giant

Words and pictures by Dylan Hewitt

Milky Way
Picture Books

Just over here

was a peaceful little place.

A little place
full of peaceful
little people

who always
helped each other,

always smiled,

**and were
always nice.**

It
was
more
than
a
little
bit
perfect.

Perfect, except for one big problem.

Well, not just a big problem...

...a giant problem.

Every day, the giant would **stomp, stomp, stomp** down to the little village and be a big brat.

When
his
giant
mouth
opened,
nothing
but
bossy
nonsense
would
tumble
out.

" Listen up,

Or I'll stomp on your whole village!"

tons of tasty treats

"Bring me

Sometimes, very rarely, the little people would muster up the courage to complain.

Just a tiny bit.

This giant bossy boots didn't have a single problem in the whole world.

"I love being a giant!" he thought.

Well, he was about to have his first problem ever.

And it wasn't a little problem either.
Or a big one. Or even a giant one. But rather...

a silly little house," a voice more booming than his own boomed.

"Oi, little person!"
the giant giant said to him.

"When I come back in the morning,
I want you to have cooked me
a feast and baked me tons
and tons of tasty treats!

Oh, and you can clean
my underwear too!"

"Or else

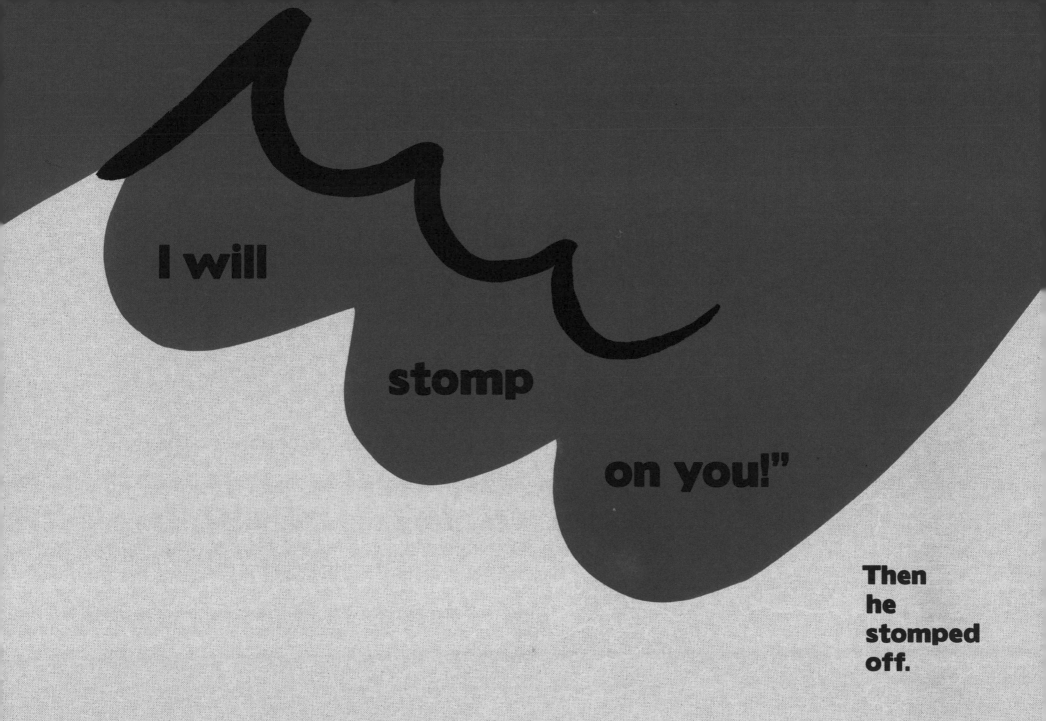

He cried his little giant eyes out. The little people could hear his whimpering and, as they were so nice, couldn't help but ask why...

And the little giant started blubbering again.

"All right, all right, stop snivelling. We've got an idea. We were going to use it on you, but I guess we can use it on the giant giant."

So, they
started
to dig
a hole.

**With the little giant's help,
they could go really deep.**

Deeper.

And deeper.

And deeper
they dug.

All night.

Until it was not
just a giant hole.

But a giant,
giant hole.

While they dug,
the little people
and the little giant
had a little moment.

"It's so much better,
helping each other!"

They all agreed.

[o] Giant

By morning, the giant, giant hole was ready.

They covered it with leaves that were just strong enough to hold the weight of the little giant.

In the distance, the sound of the giant giant's giant, giant feet could be heard pounding closer and closer.

As promised,
the giant giant returned

and
found
the
little
giant
waiting.

" Where
is
my
feast?

The little giant,
brave as can be,
replied...

"There's a tiny problem.

I haven't got any.

Guess you're just
going to have
to stomp on me."

Predictably, that made the giant giant more than a tiny bit... **furious.**

He was so angry,
he didn't just try
to stomp on
the little giant,

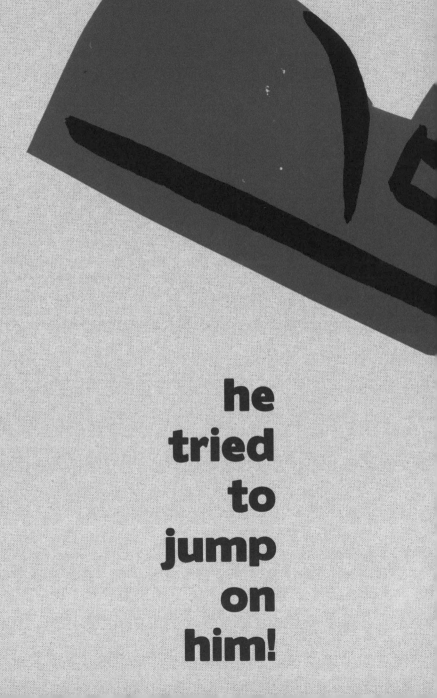

he
tried
to
jump
on
him!

But, as you know, he was about to have a giant, giant problem…

The
giant
giant
was

It didn't take long at all
before the giant giant started to…

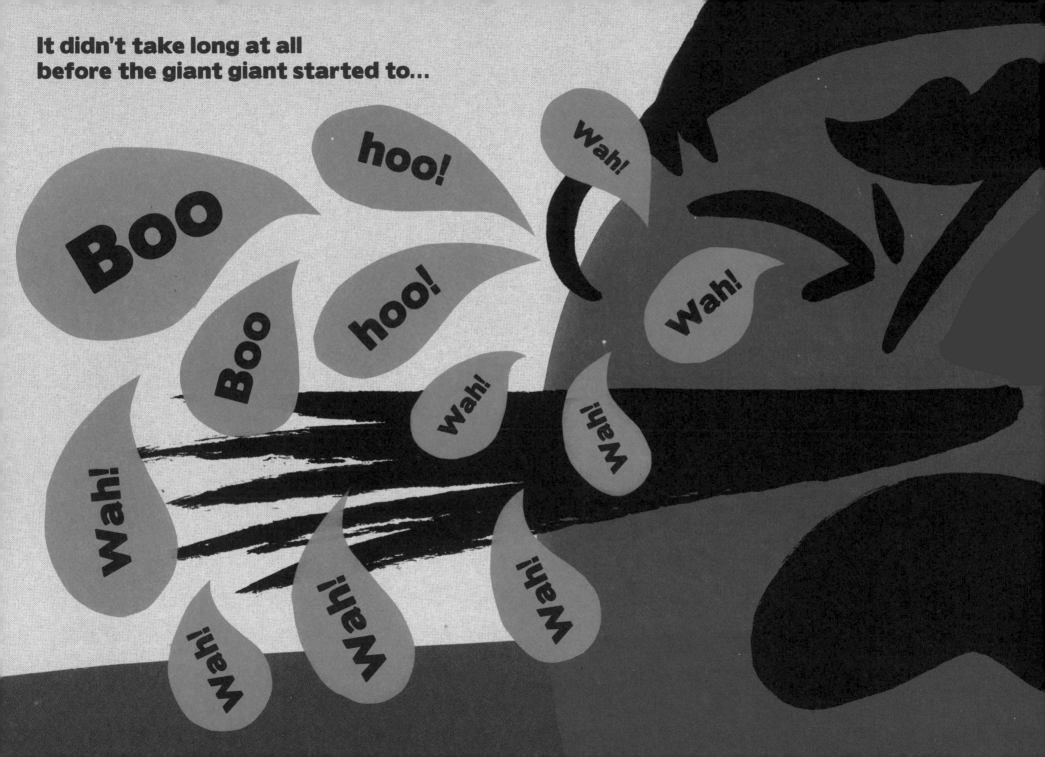

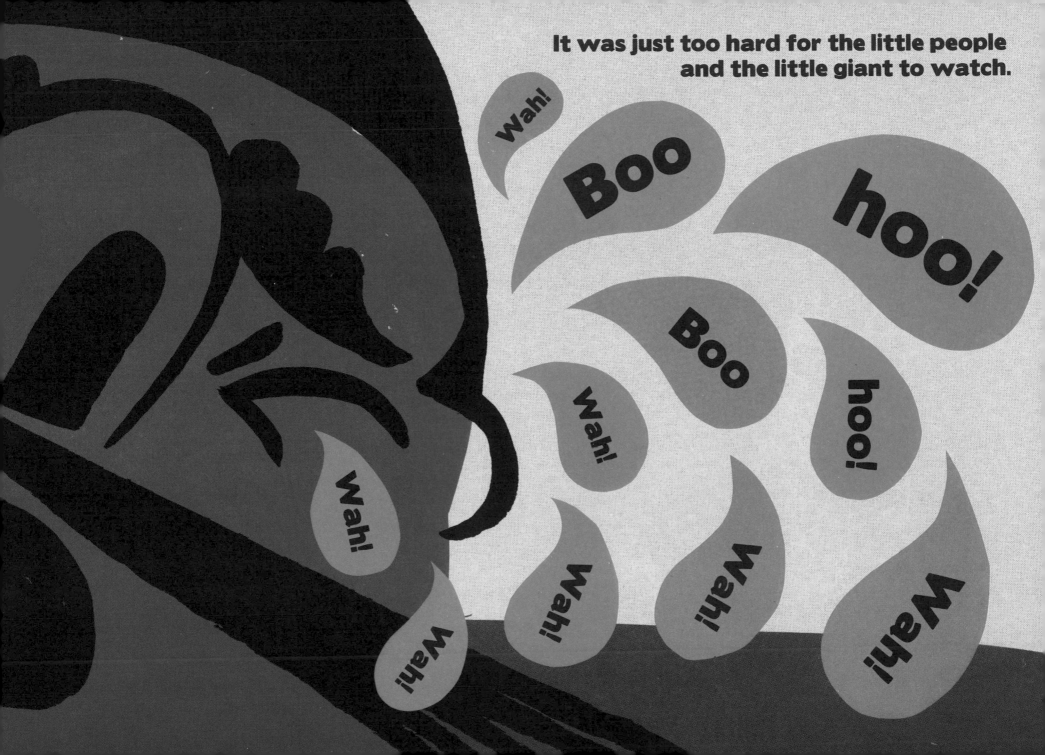

"Yes, of course!
We can be friends,"
said the peaceful little people
with the peaceful little giant.

And from that day forward,
there was...

Not one
giant problem.

not one
little problem.

It was just
a peaceful little place,
over here,

that was now more peaceful than ever.

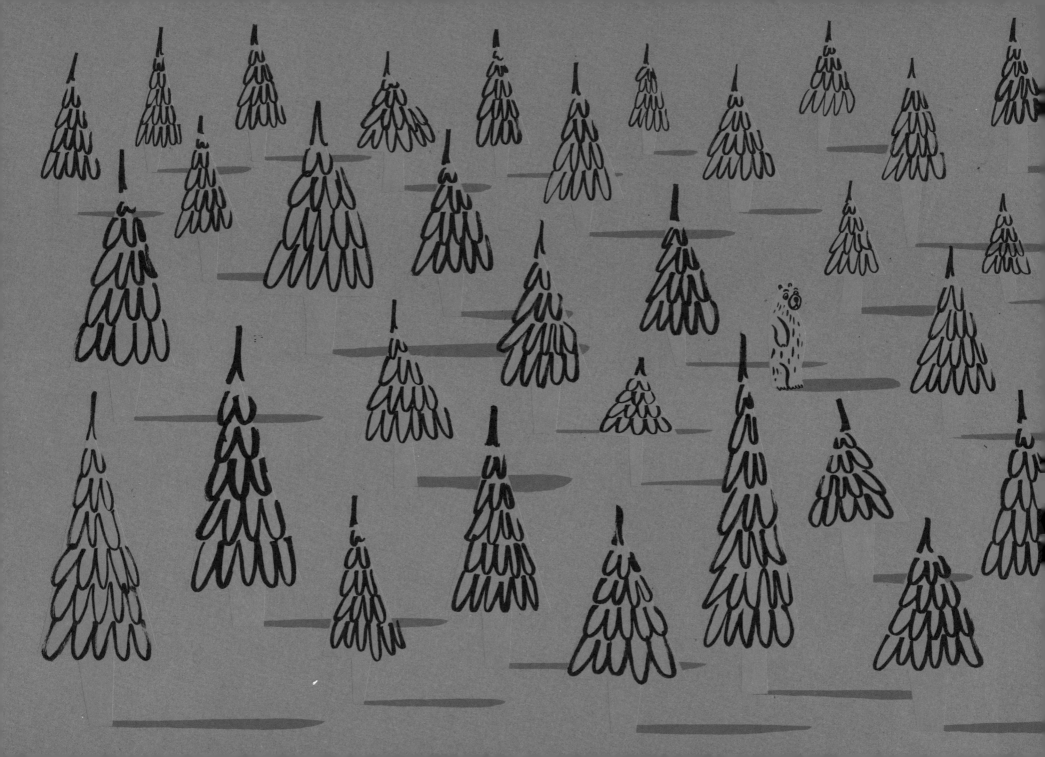